**SKYLARK CHOOSE YOUR OWN ADVENTURE® · 14**

"I DON'T LIKE CHOOSE YOUR OWN ADVENTURE® BOOKS. I *LOVE* THEM!" says Jessica Gordon, age 10. And now, kids between the ages of six and nine can choose their own adventures, too. Here's what kids have to say about the Skylark Choose Your Own Adventure® books.

"These are my favorite books because you can pick whatever choice you want—and the story is all about you."
—**Katy Alson,** *age 8*

"I love finding out how my story will end."
—**Joss Williams,** *age 9*

"I like all the illustrations!"
—**Savitri Brightfield,** *age 7*

"A six-year-old friend and I have lots of fun making the decisions together."
—**Peggy Marcus** *(adult)*

Bantam Skylark Books in the Choose Your Own
  Adventure® Series

Ask your bookseller for the books you have missed

# THE SEARCH FOR CHAMP

## SHANNON GILLIGAN

# ILLUSTRATED BY ANTHONY KRAMER

*An R.A. Montgomery Book*

A BANTAM SKYLARK BOOK®
TORONTO · NEW YORK · LONDON · SYDNEY

RL 2, 007–009

THE SEARCH FOR CHAMP

A Bantam Skylark Book / November 1983

CHOOSE YOUR OWN ADVENTURE® is a registered
trademark of Bantam Books, Inc.

Original Conception of Edward Packard

Skylark Books is a registered trademark of
Bantam Books, Inc.
Registered in U.S. Patent and Trademark Office and
elsewhere.

Front cover art by Paul Granger

ISBN 0-553-15227-0

Published simultaneously in the United States and Canada

---

Bantam Books are published by Bantam Books, Inc. Its trademark, consisting of the words "Bantam Books" and the por-
trayal of a rooster, is Registered in U.S. Patent and Trademark
Office and in other countries. Marca Registrada. Bantam
Books, Inc., 666 Fifth Avenue, New York, New York
10103.

---

PRINTED IN THE UNITED STATES OF AMERICA

CW     0 9 8 7 6 5 4 3 2 1

For Eppie Kreitner

## READ THIS FIRST!!!

Most books are about other people.

This book is about you!

What happens to you depends on what you decide to do.

Do not read this book from the first page through to the last page. Instead, start on page one and read until you come to your first choice. Then turn to the page shown and see what happens.

When you come to the end of a story, go back and start again. Every choice leads to a new adventure.

Are you ready to begin your search for Champ? Then turn to page one . . . and good luck!

You and your older sister Mag are at your **1** grandparents' summer house on Lake Champlain in Vermont. You visit the lake every summer, but this year is special. You have decided to spend your visit searching for Champ, a sea creature who lives in the lake.

Many people have spotted Champ over the years. They say that Champ has a small head with large eyes, a slender neck, and a long, snakelike body. Champ has never attacked anyone. Scientists believe that Champ is very gentle and shy. In fact, Champ is so shy that no one has ever gotten a photograph of her. Maybe you and Mag will be the first!

*Turn to page 2.*

It is a warm sunny day with only a few
clouds in the sky—a perfect day to begin.
You put on your life jackets, grab the camera,
and head for the canoe. As you look across
the lake, you realize that searching for
Champ is going to be a big job!

"Where do you want to go first?" Mag
asks. "We could go to Shelburne Point,
where some people saw Champ last summer, or we could head up toward Grande

Isle. Grande Isle might be better because there are lots of quiet, deep coves there. Remember that Champ is very shy."

---

*If you decide to go to Shelburne Point, go on to the next page.*

*If you decide to head toward Grand Isle, turn to page 18.*

**4**     You paddle your canoe toward Shelburne Point. In fifteen minutes you can see the famous house on the point.

"Let's drift for a while," Mag suggests. "It might be a good time to try out your bait."

"Good idea." You reach for a wire basket tied to a fishing line. Inside the wire basket are some large, fresh shrimp. Last year some picnickers saw Champ in a spot where they had dropped some shrimp salad out of their boat. You figure it's worth a try.

After gently letting the basket overboard, you lean back and close your eyes. The sun beats down on your bare arms. Mag hums quietly to herself. Several minutes later you feel a quick tug at the fishing line. Jolting awake, you look overboard. The water is so dark you can't see anything. Then you feel a second tug—a stronger one.

*If you pull the basket up right away, turn to page 24.*

*If you wait for another tug, turn to page 21.*

"Hey, Mag!" you say. "Let's go in and explore the place."

"Okay. I'm getting tired anyway."

You continue paddling, and after a few minutes you pull the canoe up on the sandy shore.

As you walk toward the house, a chilly wind rises. You hear a long, eerie screech. An old shutter on the second story of the house breaks off. It tumbles through the air and lands right in front of you!

You and Mag look at each other. "This place gives me the creeps," you say.

"It was just the wind," Mag says. "The house isn't haunted. That's only in the movies."

*If you decide it's safe to go inside,
turn to page 11.*

*If you decide to leave,
go on to the next page.*

**8**    "Mag, let's not go in. The house looks dangerous. Why don't we build a sand castle instead?"

Mag nods, and the two of you choose a good spot and begin work. You lose track of time. A half hour passes before you notice the house creaking in a strong wind. The skies are cloudy and dark. Thunder rumbles in the distance. A thunderstorm will start any minute.

You must do something. And fast!

*If you decide to try to head for home in the canoe, turn to page 30.*

*If you run to the high rocks at the edge of the cove and signal for help, turn to page 33.*

You shrug. Mag is probably right. The two **11** of you start off again toward the front door of the house.

The door opens when you shove it. You stumble into a dusty hallway.

"Mag, it looks as if no one has been here for years!"

"I know," she says. "Let's give it a look."

*Turn to page 13.*

You tiptoe carefully from room to room. **13**
There are pieces of broken furniture, an old
bird's nest, and *lots* of dust.

"There's nothing here. Let's go."

"Wait, Mag. Look at this." You point to a
narrow staircase behind a kitchen door. "This
looks safe. Let's explore upstairs."

*Go on to the next page.*

**14**     Mag follows you up the dark, narrow staircase. It leads to a stuffy room. You carefully look through the closet and a chest of drawers. There's nothing else but a moth-eaten bed.

But wait! Mag lifts up the mattress and finds a wooden box underneath. The box is *locked*!

You wonder what's inside.

*If you decide to take the box home and open it with your grandfather's tools, turn to page 35.*

*If you decide to open the box right now by breaking the lock with a rock, turn to page 17.*

You and Mag decide to break the lock right away. Mag runs to get a rock. She lifts it high in the air and brings it crashing down on the lock. The lock doesn't break, but the old dry wood crumbles easily. Inside the box is an old-fashioned jar of hand cream wrapped in a wrinkled green rag.

Mag frowns. "There's nothing here. Let's go look for Champ."

*If you tell Mag to go ahead while you finish looking around upstairs, turn to page 42.*

*If you want to continue your search for Champ, turn to page 46.*

**18**   You and Mag head the canoe toward Grande Isle. Out on the lake the waves are high. Your arms begin to ache from paddling, but all you can think about is getting safely across the rough waters and finding Champ.

After thirty minutes of hard paddling you are close to Grande Isle. When you are fifty feet from shore you see an old abandoned house tucked beside a quiet cove. That's funny, you think. You've never seen it before.

"Wow!" Mag shouts. "It looks like a haunted house." As she speaks, a cloud passes in front of the sun.

*Turn to page 7.*

You decide to wait before bringing up the basket of shrimp. Champ scares easily. You don't want to frighten her off.

After a few minutes, there are no more tugs. You lean back against your cushion and doze.

Mag's voice awakens you. "It looks like a storm. Don't you think we had better head in?"

"You're right. We can use the dock at Shelburne Point. That's closest."

As you paddle on, the rain starts to fall. Soon the lake is smooth from the steady pounding of the rain. It looks eerie and beautiful. The boats have all gone in to shelter, and you are alone on the lake.

*Turn to page 39.*

**22**   Sure enough, the sky is filling with dark, heavy clouds.

You point your canoe toward home and paddle with all your strength. The wind howls and the lake gets choppy and rough.

"This is dangerous, Mag. If the waves get any higher, we'll be swamped!"

"But we're almost home!" Mag yells.

You stare ahead, but you still can't see the dock. Then you glance at the shore. It looks rocky, but it might be better to pull in and wait for the storm to end.

*If you decide to continue home, turn to page 43.*

*If you tell Mag that you think it's too dangerous to continue, and you want to wait on shore, turn to page 27.*

**24**     You yank the line and peer into the dark water. No luck! The basket comes up empty. Whatever it was, it wasn't Champ. Mag looks at the dripping basket and says, "It was probably just a fish. We'd better get going, anyway. There's a storm coming."

*Turn to page 22.*

"It's getting too rough, Mag! We have to go in *now*."

You can barely hear your own voice over the wind, but Mag nods and begins to steer the canoe toward shore. The wind is at your back. It helps to push you along. You are almost there when the canoe hits a hidden rock. Water comes gushing in through a hole in the bottom and begins to fill the boat. Without another thought, you grab your camera and jump into the lake.

*Turn to page 50.*

**28**   You wake up on the shore. The storm has passed. The sun is peeking through the clouds. Mag is lying next to you, and the canoe is nearby, wedged between two rocks.

You don't remember exactly what happened. After you hit your head, you felt as if you were in a dream. You were floating facedown in the water and couldn't move. Then, out of nowhere, an enormous creature that looked like a cross between a dinosaur and a seal lifted you onto its back and swam to shore. It left you safely on the rocks.

You turned to see the creature before it left. All you saw was a small head with large blinking eyes. Was it Champ? Or were you dreaming?

Mag is awake now, too. Rubbing her eyes, she says, "You know, I think we were saved. Did you see something that looked like a huge seal bring you to shore too?"

A happy shiver races down your spine. Maybe you weren't dreaming after all!

**The End**

**30**     You and Mag launch the canoe and paddle out of the cove. The wind blows violently, and whitecaps form at the top of each wave. This is going to be rough!

The rain pours down. You've never seen such a bad storm. The waves toss your canoe about, and you are scared. A pool of water is forming in the bottom of your canoe. A big wave—then another—comes crashing into the boat. You're swamped!

*Turn to page 40.*

You and Mag run to the high rocks and scramble to the top. From here someone will see you. That is, if anyone is around.

You look for boats, but all you see are flashes of lightning. The rain is coming down hard and fast. You can't see very far. Will anybody notice you after all?

Just then you spy a boat about a half mile off. You and Mag jump up and down, waving your arms and yelling. It seems to be turning toward you, but you can't be sure.

As the boat gets closer, you can see two people wearing uniforms. It is a Lake Champlain patrol boat. You are safe!

**The End**

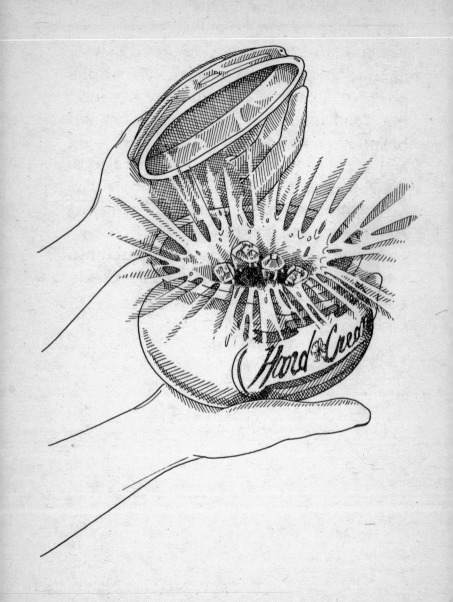

"Mag, let's take the box back and open it
with Grandpa's tools."

Mag agrees, and the two of you walk back through the house. Just as you step off the porch, your sneaker lace gets caught and you trip. The box crashes onto some rocks and breaks open. Inside there's an old green rag and an old jar of hand cream from the 1930s.

"Nothing but junk," Mag says.

"Wait, Mag. Look." You open the jar of cream. Inside are four beautiful blue-green stones.

"They look like emeralds," Mag says excitedly. "Let's go back and show them to Grandpa and Grandma."

*Go on to the next page.*

**36**    You paddle home quickly and show the stones to your grandparents. Your grandmother is sure the stones are real emeralds, so your grandfather calls the police to make a report.

Two police officers come by later that afternoon. They look at the stones. Sure enough, they're emeralds. The policemen tell you that they are from an unsolved burglary from fifty years ago.

"Where did you get them?" one of the officers asks. Your grandparents point to you and Mag.

"You've done a fine job," the officer says, smiling. "We gave up looking for these years ago. Have you two ever thought about detective work?"

"Not for now," you reply. "We have to keep looking for Champ."

## The End

Before you move any farther, you hear splashing sounds about twenty feet from shore. Looking up, you see not one but *three* sea creatures floating gracefully nearby. What great luck!

They look at you for a moment and then quickly dive back below the surface. You were so excited that you even forgot to take a picture!

Paddling home after the storm, you wonder if anyone will ever believe you.

**The End**

**40**  Just as you are about to give up, a huge figure dressed in flowing white robes appears out of the clouds. "I am a goddess, and this lake is my home. When I started this storm, I did not see you and your sister alone in your canoe. Do not worry. I will take you to shore myself."

With that, she scoops up your canoe in the palm of her hand and, smiling, deposits you safely at your dock. Before you can catch your breath to thank her, she disappears into the clouds, leaving a stream of brilliant pink light behind her.

**The End**

You'd still like to look around, so you tell Mag to go along and that you'll be out in a few minutes. After she leaves, you open the jar. Inside are four beautiful blue-green stones that look like emeralds. Maybe they *are* emeralds!

*Turn to page 44.*

Mag is probably right. You decide to continue home. You get a firm grip on your slippery paddle and set to work.

In a minute the rain begins, first softly and then in a torrent. You keep paddling, but the lake is so rough that you aren't getting anywhere. The canoe drifts dangerously close to shore.

Then there is a sudden crack—the loudest you have ever heard—and a flash of light. You are thrown from the boat. You feel a sharp pain where you hit your head on something hard.

Then . . . nothing.

*Turn to page 28.*

**44**   Suddenly, you hear Mag yelling, "Champ! Champ! I see Champ!"

You run as fast as you can downstairs. Outside, you catch a glimpse of Champ's long neck and head before she dips below the surface.

In all the excitement, you forget about the jewels until you're paddling home. You'll have to go back to get them tomorrow!

**The End**

"You're right, Mag. It's getting late, and we still haven't seen Champ."

You retrace your steps through the house. As you pass a window, you catch a glimpse of a small head, two feet above water, looking curiously at the house. It's Champ!

*Turn to page 49.*

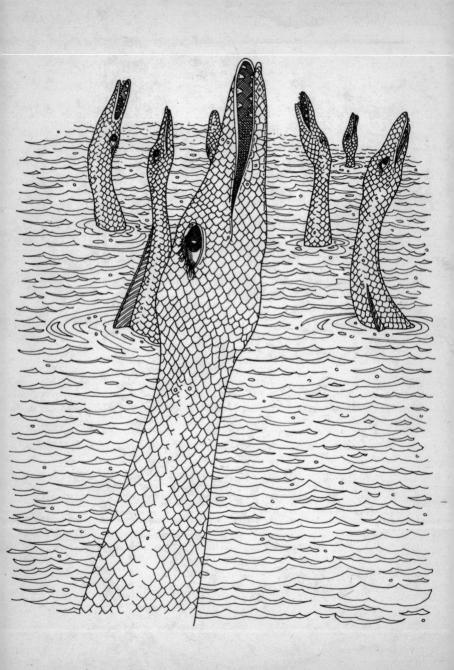

When you get outside, Champ leans her head back and cries, "Yaaooooo! Yaaooooo," in a thin, high-pitched voice. Six more creatures of different sizes—but just like Champ—appear in the cove. They stare at you and Mag for several moments. Then Champ makes another cry, and all seven disappear together, back under the surface of the water.

In a few seconds, the lake is as calm as if nothing had happened.

**The End**

**50**    You'll have to swim the rest of the way. Mag swims ahead and gets out first, helping you onto the slippery rocks. Just as you get a safe grip, Mag says, "Look! I can't believe it. Quick. GET A PICTURE!"

There, right where your canoe went down, is Champ playing in the storm. She dives in and out of the waves, splashing you with her tail. You snap your whole roll of film, twenty-four pictures in all. Wait until everyone sees these. It's lucky your camera is waterproof!

**The End**

## ABOUT THE AUTHOR

**Shannon Gilligan** graduated from Williams College in 1981. While a student, she spent a year studying at Doshisha University in Kyoto, Japan. When she's not traveling to do research for her books, she lives in Warren, Vermont.

## ABOUT THE ILLUSTRATOR

**Anthony Kramer** graduated from the Paier School of Art in Hamden, Connecticut, where he received the Children's Book Illustration award. He has been an editorial cartoonist, an architectural artist, and a designer of children's-toy packages. His illustrated books for children include *Underground Kingdom* and *Hyperspace* by Edward Packard and *Secret of the Pyramids* by Richard Brightfield, all for Bantam's Choose Your Own Adventure® series. Mr. Kramer lives in New York City, where he loves to walk, run, and bicycle.

# DO YOU LOVE
# CHOOSE YOUR OWN ADVENTURE®?
# Let your older brothers and sisters in on the fun.

You know how great CHOOSE YOUR OWN ADVENTURE® books are to read over and over again. But did you know that there are CHOOSE YOUR OWN ADVENTURE® books for older kids too? They're just as much fun as the CHOOSE YOUR OWN ADVENTURE® books you read and they're filled with the same kinds of decisions—but they're longer and have even more ways for the story to end.

So get your older brothers and sisters and anyone else you know between the ages of nine and thirteen in on the fun by introducing them to the exciting world of CHOOSE YOUR OWN ADVENTURE®.

There are over twenty CHOOSE YOUR OWN ADVENTURE® books for older kids now available wherever Bantam paperbacks are sold.

# WANT TO READ THE MOST EXCITING BOOKS AROUND?
# CHOOSE CHOOSE YOUR OWN ADVENTURE®

Everybody loves CHOOSE YOUR OWN ADVENTURE® books because the stories are about *you*. Each book is loaded with choices that only *you* can make. Instead of reading from the first page to the last page, you read until you come to your first choice. Then, depending on your decision, you turn to a new page to see what happens next. And you can keep reading and rereading CHOOSE YOUR OWN ADVENTURE® books because every choice leads to a new adventure and there are lots of different ways for the story to end.

Buy these great CHOOSE YOUR OWN ADVENTURE® books, available wherever Bantam Skylark books are sold or use the handy coupon below for ordering:

Now you can have your favorite Choose Your Own Adventure® Series in a variety of sizes. Along with the popular pocket size, Bantam has introduced the Choose Your Own Adventure® series in a Skylark edition and also in Hardcover.

Now not only do you get to decide on how you want your adventures to end, you also get to decide on what size you'd like to collect them in.

## SKYLARK EDITIONS

| | | | |
|---|---|---|---|
| ☐ | 15120 | The Circus #1  E. Packard | $1.75 |
| ☐ | 15207 | The Haunted House #2  R. A. Montgomery | $1.95 |
| ☐ | 15208 | Sunken Treasure #3  E. Packard | $1.95 |
| ☐ | 15149 | Your Very Own Robot #4  R. A. Montgomery | $1.75 |
| ☐ | 15308 | Gorga, The Space Monster #5  E. Packard | $1.95 |
| ☐ | 15309 | The Green Slime #6  S. Saunders | $1.95 |
| ☐ | 15195 | Help! You're Shrinking #5  E. Packard | $1.95 |
| ☐ | 15201 | Indian Trail #8  R. A. Montgomery | $1.95 |
| ☐ | 15191 | The Genie In the Bottle #10  J. Razzi | $1.95 |
| ☐ | 15222 | The Big Foot Mystery #11  L. Sonberg | $1.95 |
| ☐ | 15223 | The Creature From Millers Pond #12  S. Saunders | $1.95 |
| ☐ | 15226 | Jungle Safari #13  E. Packard | $1.95 |
| ☐ | 15227 | The Search For Champ #14  S. Gilligan | $1.95 |

## HARDCOVER EDITIONS

| | | | |
|---|---|---|---|
| ☐ | 05018 | Sunken Treasure  E. Packard | $6.95 |
| ☐ | 05019 | Your Very Own Robot  R. A. Montgomery | $6.95 |
| ☐ | 05031 | Gorga, The Space Monster #5  E. Packard | $7.95 |
| ☐ | 05032 | Green Slime #6  S. Saunders | $7.95 |

**Prices and availability subject to change without notice.**

Buy them at your local bookstore or use this handy coupon for ordering:

Bantam Books, Inc., Dept. AVSK, 414 East Golf Road,
Des Plaines, Ill. 60016

Please send me the books I have checked above. I am enclosing
$_____ (please add $1.25 to cover postage and handling). Send
check or money order—no cash or C.O.D.'s please.

Mr/Ms _____

Address _____

City/State _____ Zip _____

AVSK—11/83

Please allow four to six weeks for delivery. This offer expires 5/84.